STRANGER DANGER

Also by Alexandria Blaelock

SHORT STORY COLLECTIONS
The Histories of Hayward Hall
Lovelorn, Lovestruck and Love at First Sight
Common or Garden Variety Heroes
Case Files of the Wilkinson Detective Agency
Unavoidable Fates
Christmas Travesties
Five Faces of Felicia Clarke
Little Place Called Home
Security Directorate Dossiers v. 1.
Security Directorate Dossiers v. 2.

FICTION
That Love Nonsense
Taipan vs Brown
The Ghost and Ms Cox
Friends Like That
Weaving the Wildwood
Wolf vs Orb

MS BLAELOCK'S BOOKS
Stress Free Dinner Parties
Signature Wardrobe Planning
Holistic Personal Finance
Minimally Viable Housekeeping
Planning a Life Worth Living

PICTURE BOOKS
Australia Felix

SELECTED SHORT STORIES
Alma's Grace
Blood and Bloody Profanity
Cancelled by the Cartel
Dingo Hunting
Honoris Virilis Respectu
Mince Pie Mystery
Remains of Christmas

STRANGER DANGER

A FELICIA CLARKE SHORT STORY

ALEXANDRIA BLAELOCK

BlueMere Books

MELBOURNE, AUSTRALIA

For permission requests, please contact enquiries@bluemerebooks.com.

Ordering Information:
Discounts are available on quantity purchases. For details, contact orders@bluemerebooks.com.

Stranger Danger/Alexandria Blaelock
paperback ISBN: 978-1-922744-08-1
digital ISBN: 978-1-922744-09-8

Book Layout © BookDesignTemplates.com
Cover Art © Yurii Seleznov via depositphotos

STRANGER DANGER

Once upon a time, a long, long time ago, a stranger changed the course of my life forever.

For the better.

I really don't know what would have become of me if I hadn't met her.

For that matter, I don't even like to speculate.

Never before, or since, has someone had that level of impact.

I wish I knew her name, so I could thank her. Though I suppose she was old at the time, and it's been decades now.

She's probably dead.

But, it's such a shame she'll never know how much she changed my life after we met.

I think I was about fifteen at the time, sitting alone on a seat in the dog park.

The seat was hidden in a small copse of grevilleas or hakeas or something, right up the back.

Completely obscured from the gravel path winding through and around the park.

And everyone else in the park.

Or so I thought.

Outside the sun blazed, but it was cool and dark within.

A breeze had blown up outside, but inside the copse, it was quiet and still.

Aside from the soft swish of the leaves brushing against each other.

If you closed your eyes and used your imagination, it sounded like gentle waves washing up on the shore.

Though being sheltered, and in amongst the scratchy, snarly bushes, it was also alive with orange and grey spinebills flitting from branch-to-branch drinking nectar from the red and orange flowers.

Moving so fast they were just bright flashes of colour.

Chirping and tweeting as they caught up on the gossip.

It was the perfect place to hide.

At least it was if you weren't allergic to bee stings.

The drone as they floated from honey-scented flower to honey-scented flower was strangely relaxing given the danger.

And making me drowsy.

Only rarely would a dog bravely push through the bushes and bees to the inside, which had grown littered with tennis balls in varying stages of decomposition.

Sometimes I took pity on them and threw the balls over the top to a melody of delighted barks.

And sometimes I just listened to their disappointed howls.

The copse was a retreat of a kind.

I'm sure at one point the seat was out in the open before the bushes grew up around it. But it sat, seemingly forgotten by everyone.

It was the one place where I knew I was so unlikely as to see anyone as to be the perfect hideaway.

I used it a lot in those days.

Just tucked my knees up so I could rest my cheek against them and closed my eyes.

Listening to the birds and bees, and the odd car back-firing as the world carried on as usual outside.

As I enjoyed the warm, scented closeness, it was almost as if the bushes embraced me.

Kept me safe from the real world outside.

The scratchy bushes were the perfect bird sanctuary, and so it was full of birds.

I usually sat so still they shared the seat, pausing for a moment between snacks.

And going by the amount of guano, they used it a lot while I wasn't there as well.

Guano dripping down the back of the seat. Guano on the front, the arms, and the seat.

Probably more Guano on the seat than in the park itself.

Dogs included.

I read somewhere that they used to mine guano in Australia.

Mined so much of it they ruined all the coastal bird habitats. Drove the birds away from their nesting places.

Not that they cared much about that kind of thing in those days. Not like these days.

Usually I carried a large spotted handkerchief with me everywhere I went, because I'd read somewhere that large spots made you happy.

And in those days, we couldn't afford to buy tissues. Or handkerchiefs for that matter; I saved up my Christmas and birthday money to buy them, and I have never come across anyone else who did that too.

But I'd left the house in such a rush I'd left my handkerchief, and everything else that was useful there.

Including protection from the bushes in the form of jeans and a long-sleeved shirt.

So I couldn't even cover the damn seat with something to protect my clothes.

I just sat there in my tattered shorts and ripped singlet, covered in stinging scratches.

Because at the time I didn't feel like I deserved to sit anywhere other than in the guano.

Actually, let's call it what it is - shit.

I didn't feel like I deserved to sit anywhere other than in the shit.

Deep layers of stinking, wet shit.

You can probably guess I was in low spirits.

My parents had been fighting again, I don't know what about, but I assumed it had to be me.

Because I was an only child, and we didn't have any pets, so what else could it have been?

Parents are often obtuse.

And I just couldn't bear it anymore.

I snuck out while they were glaring at each other, and hightailed it to the park.

Crawling into the copse on my hands and knees because the branches were about as long as they were high and it was easier than forcing my way though upright.

As I said, the close atmosphere was like a soft, warm embrace.

Comforting.

I started crying.

Not the quiet, dignified kind you see in the movies, with tears slipping quietly down your face, but the kind of violet sobs that make an ugly noise as they wrack your whole body.

"Are you alright in there honey?" a voice asked.

I tried to be quiet so she'd go away, but at the same time, the concern in her voice made me cry harder and uglier.

So loud and self-absorbed I didn't hear her trying to get through the copse until she was in.

"Nice place you have here."

I was so surprised I started hiccupping.

The woman was old.

I thought she was must be more than one hundred, but I was young. She probably wasn't any older than sixty or seventy.

And seeing as she was at least one hundred, I was impressed she'd braved the bushes.

Though she was wearing dark blue jeans with a crease ironed down the front and a white and blue striped button-down shirt fastened at the round collar, so she was fairly well scratch proofed.

Some of her white hair had escaped from her bun and curled around her neck.

She offered me a large, pure white handkerchief with an F embroidered in blue on the corner.

I sniffed and shook my head; I knew they were precious things.

"Nonsense," she said waving it, "I have tonnes of them."

I suppose she understood I couldn't wipe my nose on my sleeve because I didn't have one.

Hesitantly, I took it.

The fabric was thick and finely woven; it was clearly expensive, yet she was offering it to a complete stranger.

A child at that.

"Blow," she said.

I looked at the handkerchief, and then at her, flicking her fingers towards me, urging me to use it.

It was like blowing my nose on a cloud.

"That's better," she said and made to sit on the other end of the seat.

"No!"

She didn't frown like my mother would have, merely raised an eyebrow in query.

"It's dirty."

"Ah," she sat down anyway, "it'll wash."

This was as unexpected as if she had taken a bath in guano.

My mother didn't like it when I got dirty.

She was always on about keeping clean, and re-spectable, and what would the neighbours think.

If she thought she had even the smallest speck of dust on her clothes she'd change them.

The woman crossed her legs, and glanced at me, but didn't say anything further.

Just looked out at what would have been the rest of the park if she could see through the shrubs.

Or maybe she was watching the birds.

And I didn't say anything either.

We sat quietly for a long time while I harried the rolled edges of the handkerchief.

Or at least it seemed like a long time, but I sup-pose it was only a couple of minutes.

She pulled a small KitKat from her pocket, sliced it open with a fingernail, snapped it in half and offered one to me.

I barely paused before I took it.

I suppose I should have been concerned about stranger danger, but she'd already offered me her handkerchief.

And a chocolate bar was nowhere near as special as a handkerchief.

Though I did wait until she'd taken a bite of her half before I nibbled at mine.

Trying to make it last.

My mother didn't believe much in chocolate either.

That's not to say I didn't love my mother, because I did.

It's just that she could be...

Well...

Difficult.

We found out later she was bipolar, which didn't make her any less difficult, but easier to deal with once we knew what was going on.

And she started taking the medication.

We ate our snack in a more or less comfortable silence.

And after a while, she asked again, "Are you alright?"

"Um, yes."

"You ran in here so fast I almost didn't believe I'd seen you."

I smiled a straight lipped smile, imagining something like The Flash streaking through the park, a blur of rainbow colour behind me.

"I was in a hurry."

"Yes, I could see that."

"My Mum..."

We sat in silence a while longer as I thought about whether I should say anything or not.

Mum didn't like it when I told tales about her.

Or at least she called them tales.

Now she's gone, I expect she was worried someone would call Child Services and I'd be taken away from her.

But you know what they say, dead men tell no tales, and I will never know now what she was thinking.

The lady waited, not saying anything, examining her fingernails.

"Sometimes we don't agree," I finally said, which seemed safe enough.

"My mother and I didn't agree at all either," the woman said, "we were too much alike in many ways."

I tried to decide whether I was like her, "I can't see it."

"I imagine when you get older you'll see it better."

I grunted noncommittally and turned my face up to the sun.

She chuckled.

I glared at her, but she was looking inwards, not at me.

"I've done so much more than my mother could ever have imagined."

"Like what?"

"I've visited every single continent, even Antarctica and the North Pole."

My jaw dropped.

"And I visited all the major art galleries from the Guggenheim in New York, to the Louvre in Paris, to the Mori Art Museum in Tokyo."

"I like art," I said, "it's my favourite subject. I want to be an artist when I grow up."

"Good for you!"

"Mum says that's ridiculous. That I'll never make a living from it and I should aim at working in a shop."

The woman smothered a snort.

I was shocked.

It had never occurred to me that Mum could be wrong about something.

"Hon, you absolutely can make a good living from art; it's not all painting pictures you know. You could work in advertising, publishing, or architecture and that's just a start.

"You can get jobs in all kinds of industries! Just check what you need to get into art college and you're on your way."

It seemed too easy.

"I'm not sure Mum would agree to that."

"Well, I can't predict what she'll say, but would you like to know what I'd do?"

I looked again at her clothes and her expensive handkerchief still clutched in my fist.

Clearly, she was successful at whatever it was she did; wearing expensive clothes and travelling all over the world.

"Okay."

"First, you need to work out all the reasons your mother won't agree with you, and then you need to research all the answers.

"And then when she tells you it's too expensive, you can tell her exactly how much it will cost, and how you might get a scholarship. And how much you can expect to earn your first year out.

"That kind of thing."

And when the woman put it like that, it was that simple.

All I had to do was find out when and where, and I'd be golden.

But I guess she could read the doubt written all over my face.

"I bet you think you're all grown up, but you've only lived a tiny fraction of your life."

Still, I frowned.

"Let's say you've lived one lifetime so far, all things being equal, you've another seven or eight lifetimes to go."

I counted out my lifetimes - she was talking about ninety years.

"That's a long time to be a shop-girl when you want to be an artist."

I tried to imagine how long ninety years was when I could barely get my head around the long, summer school holidays.

I don't remember how the rest of the conversation went, but I remember when I offered her the handkerchief back, she told me to keep it.

As a good luck charm.

I ran home, got changed, and ran to the library where the librarian helped me to research my questions.

And a few weeks later when I had the answers, I started talking to my parents about going to technical college to learn graphic design.

And I started college the next year.

Since then, I've designed all kinds of things; magazines, wallpapers, logos. You name it, I've probably designed it.

I never forgot the lady's technique for getting what I want.

I've used it for work, and in my personal life; to negotiate pay rises and contracts, as well as who does the dishes, and cleans the kitty litter tray.

That's why I framed what remains of the handkerchief, and hung it in my office to remind me where I came from.

And to pay attention to the kind advice of strangers.

To embrace the danger of the unknown.

I am, and forever will be, grateful for her intercession.

THE END

As a small token of my thanks for reading...

Please enjoy 10% off everything (excluding shipping)

at alexandriablaelock.com

with the code weatherbyten.

Turn the page for some ideas where to use it,

Do you have what it takes to be a hero?

Whether that's running into a burning building, standing up for what you know is right, or saving the Princess it's going to take everything you've got and more besides.

In this genre-spanning collection of original stories, five women draw on resources they didn't know they had.

Join them, if you dare.

Home is where the heart is

You can struggle to find the place you call home. It's not a place, it's a feeling. You'll know it when you find it.

This collection of short stories explores our search for a place we can call home.

Short, sweet and relatable, these stories will make you homesick for places you've never been.

Welcome to Wilkinson's

I'm afraid Mr Hall's running a little late, can I get you a tea or coffee while you wait?

No?

What if I tell you about some of the recent cases we've been involved in?

Get comfortable and settle in for a wild ride.

you go girl!
The opposite
of winning
isn't losing,
it's quitting.
· Martha Rosette Lutz ·
Time for
a nice cup
of tea and
a sit down
Time for
a nice cup
of tea and
a biscuit
there's a book for that

Time for a nice cup of tea
and a sit down
BEWARE THE EMPTINESS GREMLINS

Australian author Alexandria Blaelock writes mostly fantasy and mystery.

She's appeared in the Stringybark Anthology *Crowd Surfing*, *Pulphouse Fiction Magazine*, and *Ellery Queen's Mystery Magazine*.

She's also written five self-help books applying business techniques to personal matters like getting dressed, tidying up, and feeding friends.

Discover more at alexandriablaelock.com.